I0714471

ADAMINABY

Douglas Holleley

CLARELLEN

C L A R E L L E N
116 Elmwood Avenue
Rochester NY 14611

ISBN: 978-0-9707138-4-1

www.clarellen.com

NOTE: This book was initially produced as a hand-bound edition of 100 in 1998 while the author was artist in residence at the Visual Studies Workshop, Rochester, NY.

Words and Images Copyright © Douglas Holleley 1998, and again in revised form, 2008.

CONTENTS

*A*DAMINABY *is the name of a town in the Southern Highlands of New South Wales, Australia. It was submerged under a dam in the 1950's during the construction of the Snowy Mountains Scheme, a project that diverted water that formerly flowed east, westward through a series of giant tunnels and dams.*

Australians will have no difficulty pronouncing it, but it may look foreign to others. It is pronounced Addah-minnah-bee. As is the case with most Australian place names, the faster you say it, and the more you blur the syllables together, the more correct it sounds.

For Clare

IN THE BEGINNING

ONCE there was a time when there was no time. There was knowledge of the beginning and there was knowledge of the end. But there was nothing in between. Also in this timeless void, form had no boundaries or shape.

Deep in the earth there was a cave. Unlike on the surface of the planet where dreams roamed free and loose, creating and expending their potential in a continuous loop of becoming and undoing, in this cave they were trapped. As they slowly grew in shape and substance one dream would collide and attach itself to another, forming clusters of increasingly complex thoughts and images. Each of these would then merge with other clusters. This process started very slowly at first but increasingly gained in speed and momentum.

There one day came a point where these dreams coalesced into a kind of cloud and began to swirl in a circular motion. Within the cocoon of the cave, they spun faster and faster in a wild, ecstatic dance. They continued to spin and grow until finally they expanded and almost filled the cave.

It was at this point that quite an extraordinary thing occurred. From the swirling mass, flowing golden strands of energy emerged, brushing the walls of the cave. These strands conducted energy in two directions. They carried the matter that was the earth to the spinning cloud and at the same time, the coalescing thoughts and dreams were transmitted back to the earth itself. The cloud rotated faster and faster until suddenly with a loud crash, the cave was filled with light. In its center there appeared the figure of a beautiful young woman with long flowing golden hair.

She stood there for a long time—without moving or saying a word—not even thinking. She raised her arms and put her hands to her

head. As she did she became aware of herself
for the first time. With that, a rush of wind
swept through the cave like a giant sigh, opening a passage to the world above. Her consciousness was carried from the cave with this
first breath and resonated through the world.

All the swirling dreams on the surface of the
planet at this very moment, found their form.
The dreams of stars fixed themselves in the
heavens. The dreams of water filled the oceans,
lakes and rivers. Some of the dreams turned
into a myriad of different creatures. Others
formed the trees. More importantly, with this
first breath, time itself commenced—for the first
time there was a here and now. The knowledge
of the beginning and the end evaporated, and
turned instead into a strange mixture of memory
and desire lodged deeply within the soul of
every living thing.

She walked into the world. She had no
name for what she saw. We would understand
the scene as being a beautiful garden where
the plants, trees and animals lived together in
complete harmony. However, all she knew was
that she was at home. While walking she noticed a small glowing stone-like object attached
to a chain. She reached down and picked it up.
As she did it stopped glowing and turned into
purest silver. As she watched she saw a mark

appearing in the surface. The mark was in the shape of an "A" and she heard in her mind a soft voice say a single word. That word was her name. Her name was Adaminaby.

But who was Adaminaby? It is very difficult to describe her using conventional terms. Adaminaby was not so much a person as a persona. One is tempted to simply say that she was a beautiful young woman who lived in a valley under the Southern Cross. But the fact is, things are more complicated than that.

The truth is that Adaminaby was not simply an individual that lived within a particular place. She was also the spirit of that place. To help make this a little clearer, try to imagine yourself in your favorite place. This may be your room, a stretch of beach or any little secret place that when you visit it you feel at peace and at home. Try and recall what it is that you feel when you are there. If you feel secure within yourself and at the same time at one with this place then you are beginning to understand what Adaminaby's relationship with the valley was like.

Adaminaby was essentially the caretaker of this valley. All of the life of the valley, the ebb and flow of daily existence and even the passing of the seasons, were both caused by Adaminaby and reflected in her as well. It was if she was the surface of a mirror, living simultaneously as reality and its reflection, able to look out or within with equal fluency. Thus she was able to both walk through the valley as well as sense within herself all aspects of its health and welfare.

She actually had a house in the valley although it is unlikely that any normal human person could ever see it. If you could see it would look much like an English country cottage. It was quite small. There was a large kitchen with a fireplace and a table. This led to a sitting room and off this there were two other rooms, one of which she used as her bedroom and the other was there just in case. The kitchen had a door to the outside which opened onto an open porch where she would often sit in the evenings and watch the light from the setting sun flicker through the leaves of the trees that surrounded the house.

The house was constructed of hundreds of small flat stones. Each of these stones was fitted in such a way that no mortar was necessary to bind them together. They interlocked with great precision. The cracks between them were so fine it was impossible to insert even the thinnest paper. The roof was made of thatched river reeds that had dried to a golden straw color. The windows were arched and filled with a glass-like amber substance that filled the inside of the house with a glorious ethereal light.

Adaminaby's days were spent walking through the valley. As she walked the flowers and trees grew strength from her presence and simultaneously she was filled with their energy and life. On these outings the birds circled around her and the animals shyly but lovingly watched her from under the bushes and plants that grew in abundance.

Despite the fact that she appeared to be by herself she was never lonely. Her sense of belonging and inter-connectedness made such feelings impossible. Sometimes she imagined what it might be like to have a companion, particularly when she saw how the birds and other animals would form loving partnerships that lasted a lifetime. However, these thoughts quickly passed as she felt the flow of life in the valley surge through her very being. She intuitively realized that she had a relationship with the world itself that transcended even the span of a whole lifetime.

But sometimes, even so.

POSSUM

ONE night Adaminaby was sitting in her kitchen nursing a cup of tea in her hand. It was a very still night. Even though the walls of her home were solid stone, there was a strong sympathy with what was happening in the outside world. It was almost as if the stones themselves received signals from the valley and then re-transmitted them into the center of the house. There was no sense of being cut off or being denied sensation or information. On the contrary, the carefully laid stones received their subtle messages and relayed them to Adaminaby with the precision of a laser beam.

She sat there absorbed in thought when she was startled to hear a faint scratching coming from the roof. The noise was so close, and her mind so far away, that it caused her to start with surprise. She focused more closely on the noise. It was not continuous. Sometimes many minutes would pass before it started again. She was puzzled. Nothing like this had occurred before. Suddenly the sound intensified. There was a frenzy of wild scratching and even the occasional snort. She jumped to her feet and looked up to the ceiling. She could see a bulge developing right over the freshly laid table. She held her breath as the sound reached a crescendo. Without warning, the ceiling collapsed in the center of the room and a grey shape plummeted directly into the salad bowl on the table.

Leaves of lettuce and other vegetables were thrown all over the room. A particularly large circular piece of tomato was thrown onto the wall, became stuck there and then slowly peeled off to fall to the floor. The room looked like a bomb had gone off and already she was imagining how long it would take to clear up. She looked at the salad bowl. Despite the fact that large amounts of food had been propelled around the room, it still looked full. After the prolonged period of scratching and the gigantic noise made as the ceiling fell, the silence was palpable.

As she watched she noticed that the remaining leaves of lettuce were quivering on the surface. She looked more closely and could see the leaves of lettuce move more and more mysteriously within the bowl. A little paw extended from the center of the bowl to grip the rim. Shortly after another appeared. As Adaminaby watched a pink nose poked through the surface. She heard a kind of dazed groaning sound and then, as the little paws on the salad bowl tightened their grip, she saw a creature pull itself up from all the lettuce leaves.

It was a very confused and somewhat dazed possum. Adaminaby did not know whether to laugh, be concerned, or to express a certain amount of displeasure. All of these emotions were equally appropriate. The possum made an extremely comical sight. A slice of cucumber was perched on his head making him look like a disheveled sailor on shore leave. Adding to the effect, the shock of the fall made him unsteady on his feet, as he, seemingly drunkenly, struggled to find his balance. He was obviously badly shaken, possibly even hurt.

Adaminaby went to the drawer and pulled out a fresh, white tea towel. She soaked it in water and was able to get most, if not all, the bits of food from the possum's fur. She then dried him down, so much that his fur became quite buffed up and he sat there, shivering slightly, looking like a very hairy soccer ball.

Adaminaby said nothing but her quiet care and concern soon soothed the frazzled possum. Although he hadn't been asked, after a few minutes when his confidence started to return he announced.

"My name is Possum. Please forgive me for dropping in without warning."

Whether or not he had intended it to be funny, Adaminaby was shaken from her state of concern for his well-being and she burst out laughing.

"What's so funny?" said Possum, who had now recovered sufficiently to regain his sense of dignity.

Adaminaby simply replied by picking him up and giving him a giant hug.

This is how Adaminaby and Possum met and began their life together. That night, after cleaning up the kitchen and making a new supper, they sat up late together, chattering and laughing until eventually it was time to sleep. Adaminaby made a temporary bed by installing an old sideboard drawer in the second room. When she had finished she tucked Possum in soundly, gave him a gentle kiss and then went to bed.

It was with the coming of Possum that
the "salad days" began. Salad days are usually
thought of as a time of youthful innocence.
More correctly they are days where time has the
quality of being elastic enough to expand to fit
any activity. There is no rush, no panic, and no
lateness. It is unlikely that this expression comes
from Possum's descent into the bowl on Adaminaby's table, but if it did it would be appropriate.

After their unorthodox meeting the two
became the best of friends. There was always
time for each other and it seemed that simply
being with each other created time itself. The
rhythm of their day seemed to function as a
clock that guided the activities of the valley and
its inhabitants with the stability and delicacy of
a gyroscope balanced on a thread of silver.

THE FIRE

ADAMINABY and Possum developed a simple but satisfying routine. They would wake early and have breakfast on the porch outside the kitchen door. When their meal was over, they would set off on a long walk that would take them through most of the valley. As they walked Adaminaby would smile as Possum regaled her with stories of his travels. Also they both loved to reminisce about the night Possum "dropped in" for dinner.

These walks however, were not simply frivolous sociable affairs. They served an important function. Both the valley itself and Adaminaby were re-charged by each other's presence. Each was of the other and the balance of the valley was maintained as each both gave, and took, in turn from the other.

One summer morning Adaminaby and Possum went walking. The bush was electric. As they walked, the dry leaves that had fallen from the trees crackled under their feet. The very atmosphere seemed charged with energy. The heat caused the air to ripple, distorting trees in the distance as the ground radiated the rays of the sun back to the sky. Adaminaby had seen this before and was unusually withdrawn. Even the irrepressible Possum could only manage a few words before lapsing back into silence.

Late the previous evening both Adaminaby and Possum had heard thunder. Both hoped that this would bring rain to the parched valley. Instead they saw only the occasional flash of lightening and heard a distant rumbling some 20 to 30 seconds later. When the rain failed to materialize Adaminaby remembered the times that this had happened in the past.

It is actually very difficult for a fire to start without matches or some other open flame. Even if lightening strikes a tree, searing its branches and trunk with vast amounts of energy, it does not necessarily follow that a fire will be caused. Other conditions must be present. There must be sufficient kindling present to feed the scorched timber and allow the flames to develop. It must be dry. There needs to be just the right amount of wind. Unfortunately all these conditions were in place the night before.

By mid morning the valley was covered in a soft bluish-grey smoky haze. The animals and the birds were beginning to panic and even the trees seemed to be trying to hide behind each other. Paradoxically, despite the danger, the scene was extraordinarily beautiful. The light of the sun gently diffused through the smoke. The haze was so thick that it was possible to look directly at the sun itself, which despite the bluish color of the haze, assumed a beautiful golden glow and seemed to be surrounded by a vibrating halo. The light on the trees appeared to come from no particular direction. Everything was equally illuminated and glowed with a golden intensity. The green leaves of the trees looked like freshly polished bronze in both color and surface. There was only the slightest wind, just enough to cause the haze to distort the light rays in such a way as to suggest that the whole scene was occurring underwater. The trunks of the trees seemed to undulate with an almost hypnotic quality. It was if they had been mesmerized and instructed to dance to an impossibly slow but sinuous and insistent rhythm.

There was no noise. The world seemed poised in a state of suspended animation. Only the occasional mournful cry of a crow could be heard far in the distance. Adaminaby watched from her porch. This had happened before and she was filled with conflicting emotions. She knew what was to come. Worse still she knew that she could do something about it. Yet she also knew that to do so was also wrong. The calm could not, and did not last. A breeze began to cause the trees to sway and rock. The silence was replaced with a distant sound, transmitted as much through the earth itself as being carried on the wind. The sound grew and grew until eventually it became a deafening roar.

The flames first became apparent in the highest part of the trees. By this stage the fire had the forest completely within its power. The trees seemed to cringe in response to its abrasive assault. The tops of the distant trees burned fiercely. Thick green smoke curled from the tortured leaves as they exploded into flame. Like some bizarre relay race, the flaming torch was passed from one treetop to another. Each reluctant runner having no choice but to carry the burning prize long enough to pass it on to the next in line while at the same time be consumed by its savage passion.

It next came through the undergrowth. A series of burning bushes ringed Adaminaby's home. The fire then spread to the grass. The heat and flames ignited the runners that lay close to the surface of the soil. They burned and fizzled like a wick. They started at the perimeter of the clearing and appeared to aim directly for the house. They looked like fiery serpents as they snaked their way closer and closer to Adaminaby.

Adaminaby through all of this remained calm and thoughtful. Despite the destruction, she understood that the fire had its place. Many of the plants in the valley required a fire to germinate their seeds. She realized that if there were no fire then much of the valley would never regenerate. However, she was concerned that if it was allowed to burn unchecked then it might go too far, killing many animals and destroying the food for any survivors.

She began to dance. She stretched her arms above her head and stood up on her toes. She started to spin around on the spot. Her arms lowered until they were level with her shoulders. Faster and faster she spun around. She moved her arms close to her body and her speed increased to the point where she was unrecognizable. She became a shimmering blur of cool blue light in the middle of the clearing.

From the house Possum watched astonished as this occurred. He could see a hole open in the thick smoke above Adaminaby. It formed a spiral with its small point directly above her head, growing larger as it climbed into the sky. The smoke of the fire had no choice but to follow its path and was carried high into the air.

There was an enormous rush of wind. The flames were drawn by the vortex and headed skyward in pursuit of the smoke. Suddenly there was a loud explosion. It came from nowhere and everywhere at the same time and was followed by complete silence.

The fire was completely extinguished. The trees thrust their blackened branches to the now clear sky as if rejoicing and offering their thanks. The only remaining traces of the fire itself were small wisps of silvery smoke, curling silently upwards towards the sun from the tips of the charred branches.

THE ACCIDENT

ONE morning Adaminaby was troubled in her sleep. This was unusual. Almost always her dreams were gentle and peaceful as she restored both herself and her beloved valley. However, today was different. She lay in that state where sleep and the real world shimmered alternatively into focus as each fought in turn to gain her full attention.

Despite her efforts to sleep, the early morning sun and the noises outside insistently

impinged on her consciousness. Usually this
was no problem. Adaminaby enjoyed being
carried into wakefulness by the gentle breeze of
the morning and the sounds of the birds and the
animals readying themselves for the day. However, today was somehow different.

It took her some time to hear the noise. It
was a long way away and sounded a bit like a
summer cicada warming up for an extended
chant. However there was an edge to this sound
that distinguished it from normal. Adaminaby
sat up and put her feet on the floor. She noticed
that she felt slightly dizzy and sat there a moment as her head cleared. Feeling more alert
she turned her head in various directions, trying
to figure out from what direction the noise was
coming. However, as soon as she felt she had
located its direction it would either stop or become difficult to discern.

She walked across her room to the door and
shivered as her feet left her warm bedroom rug
and came in contact with the cool bees-waxed
floor. She walked through the kitchen and
opened the back door of her home. It was still
very early in the morning and when she looked
out and saw the familiar trees around her home,
their leaves playing catch with the first rays
of the sun, the strange troubled feeling began
to dissipate. She stood there, brushed by the

breeze and absorbed the beauty and tranquility
of her surroundings.

Suddenly the noise started again. This time,
being outside it was louder and sharper than
it had sounded inside the house. Adaminaby's
skin tightened and she wheeled in the direction
from which it came. Now it sounded more like
a throaty growl. Instantly she ran back into the
house and put on her green cloak. She looked
into Possum's room and could see he was still
asleep. Adaminaby was tempted to wake him
but she was worried not to lose any time, so she
quietly left the house and for the first time in a
long time made sure that the door was properly
shut.

It was obvious that the sound was a long
way in the distance. She composed herself and
began walking towards it with increasing determination. Sometimes the noise would stop for
a while and she would become unsure whether
she was still walking in the right direction. Usually however, it would start again after a few
minutes and she began to picture in her mind
where in the valley it was coming from.

She had been walking now for about an
hour. She was starting to approach one of the
sandstone cliffs that surrounded her valley and
she could hear the noise coming from one of
the deep clefts in the cliff wall. Adaminaby

knew this part of the valley very well even though she visited it only four times a year when the seasons changed. It was like a secret garden within the forest. Here there was a tree that was the only one like it in the valley. This tree was similar to a quandong, a tree that usually grew in much warmer climates than the valley.

The tree was enormous, dwarfing even the tall hardwoods that surrounded like a cocoon. It was almost as if the valley itself was the mother of this tree, or perhaps it was the other way around. It was very, very old. Its most distinguishing feature was its roots. They started growing out of the trunk of the tree about four or five feet high above the ground. As they spread from the trunk their height slowly dropped so that after about thirty feet or so they were about a foot high. These roots were like giant arms that extended from the base of the tree out into the surrounding forest. They curled around the tree in such a way that if you were able to look down on the tree from the perspective of a bird, they formed a spiral. It was in these roots, or more poetically speaking, these giant nurturing arms that Adaminaby would curl up in and dream the dream that helped the seasons to change.

Adaminaby was about a hundred feet from the tree now. The noise that had earlier seemed

like an insect was now a deafening howling
beast. It would sometimes sound like a growling
menacing dog and at other times it roared relent-
lessly like the wind and rain during an angry
winter storm.

Adaminaby stopped walking and started to
feel frightened. This is feeling she seldom had.
Her affinity with the valley had taught her that
even when bad things happened these things
were usually part of a process. Destruction,
even the death of one of her beloved animals,
she understood was part of a tapestry that
comforted the valley with a sense of continuity
as life and death flowed through the funnel of
time. However, this sound was so foreign, and
its volume so shattering, that she found herself
becoming increasingly disturbed.

She stepped off the track and slipped into
the anonymity and protection of the hardwood
forest. Slowly she crept up towards the source of
the noise. By now the sound was excruciating.
There was one last ring of hardwoods before the
clearing in which the mother tree grew and Adaminaby, her heart beating nearly as loudly as
the noise that filled the clearing, pressed herself
up against one of them as she carefully looked
around it to see what was happening.

When she looked she involuntarily cried
out. Fortunately the noise coming from the

clearing was so loud that no one heard her,
but her shock at what she saw, and how it had
made her react, caused her to duck back behind
the tree for cover. This time she steeled herself
and slowly looked at the scene again.

Adaminaby had heard about humans in the
past. Once a world-weary old crow had stayed
in the tree behind her kitchen for a few days
and in exchange for this hospitality had told her
about these creatures.

"Their numbers are many" said the crow,
"and their appetite is insatiable. They eat when
they are not hungry and divide the land with
fences. Consequently many animals become
trapped and die. If you see them you must be
very careful. They can be unbearably cruel"

Adaminaby recalled these conversations
and realized that these strangers were most
likely humans. She marveled at how much they
looked like her and she wondered for a moment
if she too was a human herself. However, the
horror of what she saw overcame such thoughts.
They had systematically cut off the arms of the
giant tree. They were now cutting into its trunk.

There were four of them. One held the
device that was making all the noise and she
could see that as he held it against the wood

of the tree, a sharp blade whirled through the wood, throwing sawdust and pieces of the tree all over the ground. The other three men did not seem to be doing much. They stood around and watched with appreciative glances the activities of the one with the saw. Occasionally they would place a thin white tube to their lips and subsequently smoke would come from their mouths. They seemed happy and in good spirits and would sometimes nod appreciatively to each other or to the one with the saw and even sometimes laugh among themselves. The saw continued to bite into the tree, which shuddered as the cut went deeper and deeper into its trunk. It began to topple. As it did the final fibers of timber stretched and ultimately broke, emitting a cry like the sound of a heart being broken.

Adaminaby realized she was crying. She felt her fear and tears however, being replaced by another emotion. She felt herself get angry.

Adaminaby instinctively understood she was powerful. She knew that the valley functioned because of her and she knew that if not for her dreams under this huge and mysterious tree, that the valley would not experience the necessary change of the seasons. It could be trapped in the dark and cold of winter, or it could be allowed to dry and die under the relentless heat of a never-ending summer. This power she intuitively exercised in rhythm with the valley and had never thought very much about it. However, she had never been angry before. How can you get angry at a storm, or even a bushfire? These things just happened. In a way they had to happen as each performed a cleansing and necessary function.

However, this was something else. She felt the tree she was hiding behind tremble as she touched it. She marveled that such a giant object could sense her presence and be affected in this way. She felt her anger mounting. As it did it created a space within her that began to fill with something foreign and strange. She fought to resist it but her tears and frustration had opened a door, allowing this force to take control.

It was at this point that things began to become unclear. Adaminaby put her hands on the tree and without pushing it, or exerting any force it began to swing and gyrate wildly. The humans were too busy looking at the fallen tree to notice what was occurring. More and more wildly the tree began to swing, so much so that the earth beneath it began to heave. Suddenly one of its roots broke free of the ground with a sound that was audible even over the noise of the powerful chainsaw. One of the men looked up and saw what was happening. He shouted at his friends and began to run away. The hardwood tree broke further from the grip of the earth spraying Adaminaby with dirt. It fell directly on the man who had started to run. Although this happened very quickly, from Adaminaby's perspective it seemed to last an eternity.

The moment the first root broke free she realized what was about to occur. She pulled back from the tree and was rocked by the earth heaving beneath her feet. With fascination she saw the hardwood almost weightlessly rise from the ground and then topple towards the man with inexorable accuracy. It did not so much as aim for the man but simply knew where to fall. Similarly the man sensed escape was impossible and his face wore an expression of fear mingled with helpless resignation as he watched the tree crash down towards him. It was almost like watching a dance.

Adaminaby's first reaction was exultation. She ran from the scene and wildly ran through the forest, hugging the trees, dancing for joy, thrilled that the horrible noise had stopped.

About an hour later she felt strangely drained and exhausted. She crept back to the scene and saw that the three men who had escaped the falling tree had pulled their companion out from underneath the tangle of branches and leaves. He was lying on his back, his head cradled in the lap of one of the other men who was caressing his forehead with a white rag dipped in water. Adaminaby felt a jolt run through her entire body as she watched this scene and tried to reconcile it with the image of indifference and cruelty that the men projected before. She could see that the other two men had fashioned a sling from the cut branches of the fallen trees and as she watched the in-jured man was strapped in and gently carried from the forest, up the walls of the valley. She watched them until they reached the top of the cliff. It took them the whole day and they did not get to the summit until sunset.

Adaminaby turned from the clearing, now a jumbled mess of sawdust, broken branches and gouged soil, and quietly walked towards home in the soft and eerily quiet twilight.

THE REMORSE

ADAMINABY walked in to her kitchen. It was a very dark night and it had taken her a long time to get home. Possum was sitting at the table. A kettle of hot water sat murmuring on the stove.

"What happened?" said Possum, who could see instantly that Adaminaby was deeply troubled.

Adaminaby explained what had occurred that day. She told him of the destruction of the giant tree and how she had frightened off the men by causing the hardwood to fall. Possum sat wide-eyed listening to the account of the adventure. He was deeply shocked by the news that the giant tree had been cut down. He understood how important it was to the rhythm of the valley and he knew that Adaminaby shared a deep and mysterious relationship with it. But at the same time he chuckled with delight as he imagined how the men must have been terrified by the events. He closed his eyes trying to visualize all the details and savored the thought of their fright and flight.

He opened his eyes to see Adaminaby crying. He knew something else had happened but was unable to imagine what it was.

Adaminaby stood up, gave Possum a kiss and went to bed. She tossed and turned in her bed and finally fell asleep. In this case she literally fell asleep. As she closed her eyes the blackness seemed to wrap around her head and then her whole body. As if weighed down by a heavy woolen blanket she felt herself become slightly dizzy and disoriented and she seemed to spiral into a void with no end. This was not particularly frightening, but as many of the experiences of the past few hours had also been, this was a new sensation.

In her dream Adaminaby was haunted by
the sound the giant tree made when it was cut
down. The groan of the timber was echoed by
the feverish cries she made in her sleep. She
dreamt of a summer that would not end and
cried in her sleep as she desperately tried to
water by hand all the trees flowers and animals
in the valley that were in her care. All night
she labored. The next morning she was quite
exhausted.

After sharing breakfast with Possum they
both went for a walk. Adaminaby was pleased
to see that the forest appeared quite normal.
Like the day before, the weather and the light
was sublimely beautiful. As the sun warmed
her clothes and body, and as the ever-cheer-
ful Possum scampered at her side, chattering
as always, she began to feel her old self. They
did their usual rounds, checking the stream that
fed the valley and making sure all the animals,
flowers, plants and trees were in order. The only
area they did not visit was the secret garden
where the encounter had occurred.

The day passed rapidly and the by now
happy and contented pair returned to the house.
That night Adaminaby's sleep was sound and
restful.

For many months they maintained this pattern and things seemed happy and normal in the valley. However, one day, for no apparent reason at all, Adaminaby was walking by herself and she heard the sound of the chainsaw again. She whirled to face the direction it came from but instantly she realized that the sound did not come from the outside world but instead from deep within her. She stopped and shook her head as if to shake the memory out. At this point another sound pushed its way into her mind. This time she heard, not the sound of the saw, but the groan of the mother tree and the sickening snap that it made as the last sinews of its flesh succumbed to the weight and collapsed. It was an awful sound. It sounded like the cry of an abandoned animal so deep was its anguish.

Almost immediately the image of the men flashed into recognition. In her mind's eye Adaminaby could see the wounded man lying on the floor of the forest. His three companions, one behind him cradling his head and the other two bending over him and wiping his forehead with a cloth seemed as sad a sight as the destruction of the great mother tree. Adaminaby had the horrible thought that perhaps they did not know what they had done.

Adaminaby was surprised by the vivid quality of these thoughts as they pushed their way into her head. She was also shocked by how painful these memories were. She gathered her strength and banished them from her mind.

However, they were not to go that easily.

It was about a week later when it happened again. This time the images and the sounds nearly overwhelmed her. In a collage that collapsed time and space, all the events of the afternoon were revisited in an instant. The experience was so vivid she gasped with surprise and stopped dead in her tracks. She was amazed at how much sympathy she had for the men. Despite the fact that they had destroyed the secret garden, and chopped down the great mother tree, Adaminaby began to regret how she had caused them so much pain. The tenderness which they had shown to each other had been a surprise at the time, but now the image of the three men gathering around the hurt man, and how their gesture formed a vague pyramidal shape, aroused in her a strange sense of familiarity and sympathy. The trouble was that this memory began to both haunt and hurt her.

She found increasingly she would imagine that she saw them in the distance. She would rush towards the vision and realize that it was just the way three bushy plants were arranged on the side of a hill, or on another occasion she thought she saw them beside the stream but it was simply three large rocks. Always when she thought she saw them she would feel the earth move under her feet as it had when the hardwood crashed towards them. She would hear the sickening sound of the mother tree collapsing and feel the rush of the hardwood tree as it unerringly aimed for the fleeing man.

She began to fear these moments. Possum who had been watching Adaminaby for some time began to worry increasingly about her. Additionally the valley itself began to subtly change. The wind no longer danced through the leaves of the trees. Now it had a discernible edge to it. The leaves shuddered and sometimes appeared to recoil from its advances. The colors in the flowers changed slightly as if in sympathy with the leaves. The days were still sunny, but the warmth of the sun began to change. Rather than diminish, the sun became noticeably more intense. It shone down on the valley with an almost cruel indifference causing the trees and plants to gasp for relief from its relentless gaze. Adaminaby noticed these changes herself.

Increasingly she felt a gulf opening up between herself and her beloved valley. A splitting was beginning to occur and she felt herself begin to separate and lose the deep connection that she once felt with the world around her.

Sometimes she would be her old self and feel the wind, the sun and the forces of life in the valley coursing through her as they did in the past. However, always this feeling would come to an end as the image of that awful day suddenly intruded into her mind with the suddenness of an exploding firecracker.

She would try and talk herself out of the black moods that were caused by these episodes. She found herself arguing with herself as she took her daily walk. The birds in the trees and the animals who watched her tenderly would sometimes take fright as Adaminaby would suddenly cry out or simply begin talking to herself as if deep in conversation with another person who could be neither seen nor heard, but who obviously had Adaminaby's complete attention at that moment.

The entire valley watched and waited to see what would happen next.

THE FLOOD

I T started a little over a year since "the accident." It began as a normal day—breakfast,
a chat with Possum and getting dressed for the
morning walk. After leaving the house Adaminaby walked down to the stream that flowed
through the valley and stopped in her tracks. Although it had not rained now for over a month,
the stream was beginning to rise. The water was
lapping over the banks, and some of the small
flowers which once grew alongside the water
were now sticking their heads up through it in
such a way that it appeared they were growing
out of the stream itself.

She was puzzled by this development. It made no sense that the water should rise without rain to feed the stream. She began to walk downstream. The further she walked the deeper the water became. After a mile or so the water was beginning to look like a small lake. Admittedly, it was not very deep, and it looked much like it did after a heavy rainfall, but it was worrying all the same.

Like the day of "the accident," the drama was accompanied by a sound. However, instead of the growl of a chainsaw, this time Adaminaby heard a persistent and rhythmic thumping noise. It went thunk….thunk….thunk. It continued in this manner without any break in the pattern. She listened for a long time, trying to imagine what might be responsible for this sound. After her last experience she was far more cautious about approaching anything new and different and she waited patiently, proceeding no further until around five in the afternoon when the noise abruptly stopped.

Even then Adaminaby was careful. She waited for about an hour and then resumed her walk downstream. It was starting to get dark and the expanse of water seemed strangely beautiful as it reflected the sky and clouds. However, as the sun continued to set, the bright colors in the water dissolved into an ominous steely grey.

Without the heat of the sun the water radiated
an almost unearthly chill.

She shivered a little but determined to
keep walking. Suddenly the source of the noise
became apparent. There was a large yellow
device, probably a kind of tractor, with a crane
that held in position a smoothly milled log. This
device was so arranged that a piston attached
to the crane was capable of driving this huge
log deeply into the ground. Adaminaby could
see that many logs had already been hammered
into the ground to form a giant fence across
the stream. Other logs had been placed against
these posts and vast amounts of soil had been
somehow pushed up against this intrusive structure. Everywhere were the tracks of humans and
of heavy machinery.

Adaminaby was deeply shocked to see this
sight. Her first impulse was to use her power
to destroy the structure but she could not bring
herself to exert her will any more. The experience with the mother tree had taken its toll and
she felt shaken and slightly weak.

She climbed on to the top of the wall and
began to scrape at the earth with her bare
hands. She spent many hours tearing at it until
she cried with exhaustion and frustration. She
stood up and walked backwards to look at her
work. She had been able to carve a small chan-

nel in the wall about two feet wide and about three feet deep. It was amazing that she had been able to make any impression on the structure at all. Her hands were cut and bruised and her clothes were a mess. She pushed her hair back off her face with the heel of her hand and in doing so smeared herself with mud.

It must have been close to the middle of the night when she had no choice but to stop work. She watched as a small dribble of water passed through the channel she had made and turned her back on her efforts. Half walking, half staggering she made her way home.

Possum was waiting up for her when she arrived home. When she walked into the kitchen she was barely recognizable. Her clothes were torn and she was covered with mud. For a moment Possum stared in disbelief as he both recognized her but simultaneously was struck by how strangely different she looked.

"What happened?" he cried. "You must get clean straight away!"

Possum scampered upstairs and ran a bath then rushed back down to help Adaminaby. He made her a cup of tea and prepared some hot and delicious soup. Adaminaby sat mournfully on the chair saying nothing. Her elbow rested on the table and she cradled her head in her hand. She seemed oblivious to the dirt on her clothes, hands and face. She stared blankly at the opposite wall of the kitchen.

Despite the delightful aroma of the soup, Adaminaby was reluctant, or unable, to eat. Possum sat patiently beside her and scooped a small portion from the bowl and put it to her lips. At this tender gesture Adaminaby smiled weakly and seemed to somehow re-enter herself. With a deep sigh she drank the offered soup and after a few more sips was able to look at, and talk to, her faithful friend.

Adaminaby told Possum about the dreadful sight she had seen and her efforts to remove the dam from the path of the stream. Possum was a little nonplussed. He knew Adaminaby could dismiss the structure with a wave of her hand if she only had the will. He was aware however, that something had happened to her ever since the day at the secret garden. This knowledge only increased his concern. He was however, sensitive enough to realize that saying anything to Adaminaby at this stage would not help matters.

Adaminaby eventually finished her soup. She was too tired to drink the tea however, and with Possum's help she slowly climbed the staircase and lowered herself into the bath. The warm water dissolved the mud and for a brief moment it even seemed to dissolve her fears.

Adaminaby could not help thinking how the water in her bath was the same water that was now beginning to flood the valley. It struck her as strange that the same substance was equally capable of making her dirty as well as clean, but such reflections were quickly overcome by the terrible tiredness brought on by her efforts. She had barely enough energy left to dry herself before tumbling into bed.

The next day she and Possum went for a walk towards the dam. They could hear the same sound as before. Thunk….thunk….thunk. They exchanged grim glances and crept up through the bushes to see what was going on. There was a frenzy of activity occurring at the dam wall. The yellow machine was driving poles into the ground with rhythmic persistence. Other machines fitted with giant blades pushed the soil up between the posts, further cutting off the flow of the stream. Adaminaby and Possum were horrified to see such energy and determination.

"Don't they realize how important the stream is?" whispered Possum.

Adaminaby could only shake her head sadly as the wall got higher and higher as they sat and watched.

After what must have been many hours the two walked back to the house. They sat down

in silence. Possum was tempted to encourage
Adaminaby to destroy the structure. In fact he
started to say so a couple of times. But each
time he had worked up the courage, he could
not get the words out when he saw how de-
jected she appeared. Possum was worried about
the dam, but even more he was worried about
Adaminaby.

The days dragged on and on. The progress
of the dam was frighteningly fast. It was like
being trapped in a bad dream where images
raced in and out of view and there was nothing
that you could do but simply stare with grim
fascination. The work continued for one cycle of
the moon and the water level grew slowly but
continually each day. Then it began to rain.

There had been a dry spell in the valley.
Dust had accumulated on the leaves of the trees
and bushes and when the rain first appeared
every living thing in the valley welcomed it. The
tired trees were washed clean and the animals
no longer needed to walk to the stream to drink.
There were sparkling pools of deep fresh water
everywhere and the forest began to revitalize
itself. Even better was the fact that the noise of
the men working on the dam had stopped and
the bush was again able to enjoy its own sweet
sounds.

Both Possum and Adaminaby hoped that this would be the end of the noise forever. They even entertained the thought that the work might somehow disappear and things would return to normal. They chattered to each other as they discussed this possibility and Possum was relieved to see Adaminaby begin to smile again.

However, the rain refused to stop. It pelted the valley with a ferocious persistence. It was so intense that neither Possum nor Adaminaby were able to go outside at all. Instead they stayed in the kitchen, wondering when it was going to end.

It was late in the evening of the fortieth night of continual rain. Possum was idly sitting at the table with his feet somewhat impolitely resting on the tablecloth. He looked down and saw water coming under the door of the kitchen. Without thinking he jumped to his feet and opened the door. A wave of water entered the room. It swirled through the kitchen, upsetting the empty chairs in the room. Brooms, food bowls and all manner of things floated on the rushing water and were carried into the rest of the house. It was a mess. The water was already knee deep and Adaminaby and Possum struggled through the torrent to make their way outside.

Outside the full moon broke through the cloud cover to reveal the fact that the entire

valley was completely flooded. Adaminaby
felt her heart sink. Instinctively she knew she
should run for the safety of the cliffs that surrounded the valley but instead she picked up
Possum and started to half wade, half swim, in
the direction of the dam. The going was very
tough as the moon would shine for only a few
minutes before the clouds would swirl back,
plunging the valley into darkness. Possum was
terrified and clung desperately to Adaminaby's
neck as she forced her way through the swirling
current. The going was getting very dangerous.
Large pieces of wood rushed past the pair as
they struggled to maintain their footing. More
than once Adaminaby tripped on some unseen
obstacle and they were both plunged underwater to re-emerge coughing and spluttering.

Adaminaby was just regretting bringing Possum with her when a large wave, whipped up
by the wind, came from nowhere and threw the
pair completely off balance. Possum lost his grip
on Adaminaby and was carried off in the swirling current. Adaminaby heard his cries in the
darkness and struggled to catch up with him.
However, the force of the current was too strong
and Possum's voice, desperately calling for Adaminaby could be heard fading in the distance
to be eventually completely drowned out by the
sound of the rushing water.

Adaminaby's heart sank. Even in the middle of all the confusion she could not help but think that all this started on the day in the secret garden. She struggled to her feet and was able to climb onto a rocky outcrop. Again the moon briefly shone through the clouds and she was able to survey what remained of her once beautiful valley.

It had turned into a vast lake that stretched in every direction. Hemmed in by the walls of the cliffs the water swirled over all but the highest trees. Adaminaby felt the last of her resistance crumble and she began to cry. She felt herself just simply let go and experienced an extraordinary sense of peace pass over her. Her tears mingled with the water and she felt herself begin to dissolve. All sense of her body left her and her consciousness began to merge with the rising water. Previously she was both in and of the valley, now she was in and of the lake

Instantly it stopped raining. The wind dropped and an unearthly calm descended over the lake. The sky cleared and the moon shone on the lake with an icy intensity turning it into a giant mirror. From the heavens, the stars of the Milky Way and the Southern Cross saw themselves reflected, their miniature image looking like a newly exposed diamond washed from the clinging earth.

THE ARTIST

Most of the creatures in the valley, and certainly all of the trees, were destroyed that evening. Possum was one of the few to escape. He was terrified as he struggled to stay afloat in the maelstrom. In the darkness he was able to climb on a large log that floated in the water and he clung desperately to it all night long. In the morning he realized that his raft was the trunk of the mother tree that had been cut down by the men. He stayed on the tree until it finally bumped softly into the earth just near the wall of the dam.

Many years passed and people came to live by the lake that was once the valley. The water helped these settlers grow crops and water their farm animals but it had a strange quality. It was both slightly sweet and slightly salty. The settlers gained peace from the lake because it was always so calm—and at night some swore they heard a young girl singing in the distance.

This phenomenon was so persistent that scientists came to investigate. They found nothing of course. Various explanations were proposed. Some said it was the winds whistling through the cracks in the cliffs. Others said it was the sound the water made as it poured through the causeway of the dam. Some folks even muttered about it being a ghost. The fact is that it was simply a mystery and like all mysteries needed no explanation to justify its existence.

Eventually even the settlers went away. They had squandered the water on their crops, raising the water table in the earth to the point that their crops either drowned in the ground or failed to mature. They left behind their homes and sheds which eventually weathered and collapsed leaving only the occasional chimney defiantly standing among the rubble of their former homes and dreams.

One day an artist came to the deserted
lake. He saw the trunk of a huge tree lying on a
sandy beach that had formed near the dam. He
pitched a sheet of canvas over the trunk of the
tree and spent the night on the beach, lying next
to its giant form. That evening he dreamed of a
time when the lake was not a lake but instead
the most beautiful paradise full of animals and
flowers. The next morning, almost in a trance
he took his small axe and began to chop at the
wood.

It is said that in the past a certain sculptor
claimed that he was not carving a figure, but
instead revealing a form already locked within
the block of stone. This was certainly the case
with this artist. He felt his hands move, and his
blows modified, by a strange force. Sometimes
he would attack the log fiercely and other times
he would delicately shave razor thin shards from
its timber.

He spent many weeks at the beach. He had
not come prepared to do such work and had
only his small camp axe to work with. He also
had very little food. However, each morning
he would awake to find small piles of nuts and
other bush fruit placed carefully in small piles
outside his tent. Strangely he never got lonely
at night. Often, just as he was falling asleep, he
imagined he could hear the most beautiful song

being sung by someone on the other side of the lake. He realized of course that it was just his imagination. He felt so foolish when one day he took a break from his labors and walked over the dam wall to the other side of the lake to see if he could see if anyone was there. All he found was a small silvery locket with the initial "A" engraved on it with a particularly delicate handwriting. He placed it in his pocket and returned to his camp.

His presence was a calming influence on the place. All the animals welcomed him. In particular a young, bright-eyed possum would watch as he worked from sun up to dusk.

One day the sculpture was finished to his satisfaction. The flowing lines and the carefully polished surfaces of the sculpture gleamed softly in the late afternoon sun. The artist was surprised that with so few resources he had been able to make such a beautiful and highly finished piece of work. He looked admiringly, but not proudly, at how he had been able to carve it all with his simple axe. He was also glad he had learned to burnish the surface with other harder woods and then polish it to a soft lustrous finish with beeswax he had found in an abandoned hive.

He slowly walked around the sculpture, which even though he had made with his own two hands, was still somewhat of a surprise to him. Usually when he worked he made sketches and worked out most of the appearance of the work in some detail before he even started. He could not remember when he had ever simply just made a something from scratch with no clear and fixed idea in mind.

As he looked at his work he felt the sensation of attachment he had for many of his creations. He was shy to admit it but he loved making art and loved enjoying his work when it was finished. Quite often it seemed to have a life all its own. However, his attachment to this piece was stronger than usual. It possessed an aura of singular individuality. It seemed so real. He looked at the serene face and the beautiful body of the young girl and wondered who she might be.

www.ingramcontent.com/pod-product-compliance
Lightning Source LLC
Chambersburg PA
CBHW041411010726
47507CB00001B/75